∽ Allister ∽

Allister

Shelley L. Houston

JUST
DUST
PUBLISHERS

Just Dust Publishers
PO Box 24312
Eugene, OR 97402
JustDustPublishers.com

Cover design and interior design and layout:
Cretia Prout, onlinedesign@comcast.net
Cover watercolor:
Wendy Bachmeier, WendyBachmeier@gmail.com
Inside illustrations:
Shelley L. Houston, Wendy Bachmeier, and Gwen Philipsen

Dedicated to all my grandchildren.
May you always be Light bearers.
I love you,
Grammy

With special thanks to:
My devoted friend, Gwen Philipsen (Ms.P) who
challenged me to write this book and assisted me
numerous times, in countless ways, to bring it to print;
To faithful friends who helped edit including my mama,
Ian Houston, and Dusti Johnson.
To my children, Stephen, Ian, and Brielle who have
taught me much while providing endless material
about which to write;
To M.S.H., my sweet husband, Mark, who continually
supports and believes in me;
And most importantly, to my Lord Jesus Christ,whom I
love with all of my heart.

Soli Deo Gloria

— 1 —

The night Allister was born a star of promise twinkled in the heavens. Some might think a mere mouse has no angel to watch their ways, but think again. The Creator of the universe holds every atom, every element of nature, in His hand—and molds them together to make every living thing. So, to set an amazing path for one tiny mouse is easier for God than a twitch of an eye. Don't doubt that.

And Allister's way was set to shine. Not that his mouse family or the community in which Allister lived understood just how special he was. Not at all. In fact, because he was the runt of the litter, many in the community made fun of him. Other young mice would sometimes call him names like "Allie-oops" when he dropped something heavy. Some mean micettes would whisper the insult of *Alley Cat* when no adult mice were around.

Nevertheless, the Creator had placed a strong heart in Allister, and he survived his frail stature and the taunts of the other mice. Instead of withering at cruel remarks, each comment seemed to feed his will to achieve in life.

He grew to be a tough little mouse, bent on being the best he could be, which is good. But sometimes, he even wanted to be better than everyone else, which is bad. One of those times, Allister fell into thinking about how he could be better than all of the other he-mice in his mouse community.

First, you should know that the mice lived in the walls of McAllister Elementary School in Trinity, Illinois. Allister and his young he-mouse friends went on food hunts for their families. It had been a long dry summer. Since there were no children eating their lunches, the mice had been scrounging for months for any crumbs they could find.

But now September had come, and school would start tomorrow. That meant that people's children would soon be bringing new lunch boxes full of food, which when they ate, would leave crumbles for the mice to gather after the people were gone.

The young he-mice were ecstatic at the idea of fresh food. They released some of their excitement by playing games in the basement before they went home from food gathering. One of Allister's favorite games to play with his friends was a game called "Chicken." That's when he got that idea— that he could become the best mouse in the community.

Allister explained the game to his father that night before school started. They were at home under one of the cupboards in the school's kitchen.

"It's just not going to happen," his father, Duke, said as he paced their newspaper floor. "No son of mine is going to be taking foolish risks."

"But, Dad," Allister said, "all the guys do it, and no one has ever been caught."

Melba, his mother, shook her head. "I suppose if they all jumped off a table..." Mother began.

"Mo-THER!" Allister interrupted. "I promise you, nothing is going to happen."

"Roll my eyeballs!" exclaimed Elizabeth, Allister's sister.

Allister turned sharply to look at his sister. "What's that supposed to mean, Lizard Breath?"

"'Elizabeth' to you, Alli-sissy," his sister replied.

"Micettes!" Mother scolded them both. She turned to Allister. "Your sister has been studying men's children. She has noted that they respond in an odd way on occasion by rolling their eyes instead of giving a verbal answer." Mother spoke with pride dripping from her voice.

"They especially do it when someone says something stupid," Elizabeth added.

Mother turned to give her a warning look but said, "Of course, we don't have whites to our eyes, so we can't really 'roll our eyes'; not and be noticed. Hence, Lizzie, or, ah, Elizabeth has adopted the expression."

Thinking his dad was reading the carpet, Allister stuck out his tongue at Elizabeth. When his mother finished her explanation Allister murmured, "Well, roll my eyeballs."

Mother looked at him sharply, and he cowered before her saying, "I was just trying it." Suddenly, Allister was airborne and helplessly hanging by the scruff of the neck in his father's clasp.

Duke held Allister eye to eye. "I certainly hope no disrespect was intended toward your mother."

"No, Father." Allister's voice squeaked out the answer, and his bad attitude evaporated.

Mother and Elizabeth busily set to

work on dinner. The meal unfolded with its usual melee of activity—especially since the baby quintuplets needed to be fed and bedded. Allister's five little brothers were each the size of a peanut and shiny pink in color. Everyone worked together until the regular deep breathing of the sleeping baby mice serenaded the house. Mother and Elizabeth relaxed in the corner, sharing whispers as they shredded straw for fresh bedding.

Allister felt strangely left out. "Where's Dad?" he asked.

"I think he's gone to say his evening prayers," Mother answered.

Allister was glad to be out of the cafeteria cupboard. He scurried through the mouseways to the roof of the old school house. Leaning back, Duke stared heavenward, hands tucked behind his head, knees crossed over the gutter's edge.

Allister approached him reverently. "Dad?"

"Allister." His father's voice welcomed him. Duke held out an arm for Allister to snuggle at his chest, which he did. Allister could hear his father's heart beating.

Duke didn't take his eyes from the array of wonder above them. Somehow, the sky was unusually grand; every star twinkled with a glorious light. "This night's sky is amazing, isn't it?" Duke asked.

Allister stared and whispered, "Yeah."

"Some of the ancients say that on a night like this, a mouse can talk to the Creator who made us."

A warm moment of awe pulsed between them, but then Allister squirmed. "Dad," he said. "I just wanted to explain about the game..."

No response.

"I'm not sure how it all got started. The guys and I were just on a normal run for food one night when we got to laughing about the cat, Milton, being so stupid. You know what a fat, lazy rump he is!"

"Don't be crude, Allister." Father still searched the sky.

"Sorry, Dad," Allister backpedaled. "Anyway, we got to thinking how fun it would be—and totally harmless—to play a game of Keep-Away from Milton. The last one to leave the playing field wins. He's the best. The big winner, Dad.

"Or he loses his life," added Father.

"Oh, no." Allister snickered. "Milton's such a wimp. Besides, I've got him totally figured. You see, he always comes through that noisy cat door and then walks slowly down the basement stairs like he's a robot. I guess he's tired from a long night. It isn't until he hits the third step from the bottom that he even sees us at our assigned posts around the floor."

"Allister," Dad said, but Allister was so wound up that he went on.

"Usually, Dillon is so scared by then that he takes off running. Milton jumps for him first, but Dillon is always stationed farthest away. The rest of us do cat calls, run around Milton, between his legs, and sometimes we even pull his tail. Ha! That always gets him to turn. By the time he regains his focus, we've run up the wall and are safely hidden in the mouseway, laughing our heads off. It's a blast!" Allister could not help but laugh at his own story.

However, Duke was not amused. "Why are you persisting in this?" he asked.

Allister sobered. "Well, Charles Lindstrom...You remember that new family in the lavatory wall? Well, Charlie thinks he is so cool. The last time we played, he was the last one home. Julian said I was next to last—a loser."

"Julian?" asked Father.

"He's the lookout and referee."

"Of course." There was a long silence. Then Duke spoke. "I understand what you're feeling, Allister. But the answer is 'no.' You're wrong in thinking that winning this game will make you better than other he-mice. It won't.   Perhaps you can't understand this now. Just trust me."

2

The food gathering went without incident, and the young he-mice met before returning home for a quick game—of Chicken.

Dawn shot eerie rays through the

basement windows of the school where Allister trembled in the dark. He imagined giant cats and other monsters shape-shifting in the shadows on the basement wall. He forced himself to look away. This was no time for fraidy-cat thinking.

Allister's pink ears acted like sonar receptors as his gaze swept the mice stationed around him. To his right, Dillon and Bob were crouched, frozen, as if in starting blocks. Dillon vibrated with tension. Allister marveled briefly that Dillon's whiskers shook so fast they looked like they were rotating.

"Come on, kitty, kitty," Dillon growled. "If I don't get home soon, Papa will find me missing, and that will mean curtains." He finished dramatically slicing the air with his finger across his neck.

"Whas-sa-matta' Dilly Bar?" Charlie snorted. "You chick'n?"

The fur stood high on Allister's back. "I wish that kid would move back to the alley he came from," he muttered.

Directly in front of Allister, Charlie glided on all fours. His shoulders hunched, his tail dragged, and his chin jutted as he jawed a wad of gum. His eyelids pulsed nonchalantly with each smack.

He thinks he's *so* cool, thought Allister, but from the sharp cock of Charlie's ears, Allister knew that Charlie only pretended to be calm.

Allister turned to look left. Willy had frozen there in a most peculiar pose. Ready for a chase, his nose stretched skyward and north while his tail stretched skyward and south.

Allister suddenly realized that Willy's stance would make him a perfect fountain if water poured from his large ears and mouth.

A wild giggle bubbled up from Allister's tummy, but he clamped a paw over his mouth to squelch the runaway laughter.

Just then, Julian, the referee, blew a sharp whistle between his teeth. "OK, relax mice-men," his voice called out from the lookout post, "the MEW has landed."

MEW was a nickname they gave the cat. It meant "Milton Eats Worms." And when Julian said the MEW had "landed," he meant that the cat had sat down, stopping his approach to the basement. Oh, they all knew this was temporary.

Milton did whatever cats do when they venture out at night, but no cat would put his life in jeopardy by being around a schoolyard during the day—especially the first day of school. And even though Milton's lack of brain cells was a humorous subject among the young he-mice community, everyone knew Milton would find his way back to safety in the basement soon after the sun rose.

The boys began to complain, "This is so typical!" spouted Bob.

Allister added, "Milton is so lazy, he can only walk ten feet before he has to rest."

"Come on, guys, stop the chatter," Willy warned. "You know the rules. Only the ref can talk." Willy's love of order stopped them short.

All eyes ascended to Julian standing at the window lookout. His arms were crossed squarely over his chest, his face grim. Silence did follow.

No one ever argued with Julian for his post. Authority oozed from his pores as naturally as the oil that gave his black fur a leather-like sheen. Julian turned again to watch for Milton.

Allister relaxed his stance. His mind wandered back to last night's dinner when his father told him he could not play Chicken anymore with his friends. Allister's guilty memory ended abruptly with the warning call from Julian.

"It's show-time!" The lookout's call echoed against the concrete walls, and the game of Chicken began again.

Adrenaline revved Allister's engines. Every tail in the basement became an antenna.

Milton was on the move.

FLA-CLAP! The cat door slammed shut. Panic rippled over the competitors faster than the echo that followed. The landing squeaked softly under Milton's weight. Every eye unblinking, focused on the staircase, but shadows hid the top of the stairs. The silence grew thick with tension.

Where was he?

Allister shot a quick look at Dillon whose shaking was now audible as his teeth hit together, sounding like a drum roll of suspense.

Something's wrong, thought Allister.

The streak slammed on top of them before their next breath. Milton's forepaws pinned down Bob and Willy. Horrible squeals filled the room with terror. Confusion ran the mice into each other in their efforts to escape. Allister's mind grasped the situation

19

first. "Attack!" he countered.

Dillon unglued from the floor. His chattering turned to a strange war chant. He rushed Milton's tail. "Whoop-whoop-wee!" he yelled.

Finding courage in Dillon's advance, Allister jumped on top of Milton's head. As Allister grabbed Milton's right ear, he yelled to Julian for help. Julian shot down the wall and began a ping-pong run just out of Milton's reach.

In miraculous harmony, Allister and Dillon chomped mightily on both ends of the cat. His eyes bulged! He hissed and shook his head, trying to dislodge Allister.

Willy strained to turn and bite hard on the paw that held him. Bob copied Willy and chomped on Milton's mitt.

"EEE-MA-OOW!" Milton cried in pain as he jerked back his feet. He turned to snap at Dillon, but too late. Milton clawed furiously at the top of his own head with both claws, only to scratch his already bleeding ear.

Allister bounded, untouched, to the floor. He leaped to the concrete wall and ran up a crack, following his friend's run to safety. Milton cried and ran furiously toward the mice. He jumped up the wall and twisted in the air to make a final swipe at Allister. One of Milton's claws just ripped a small tear in Allister's tail as he ducked into the mouse-hole. Safe!

All the boys panted heavily as they collapsed inside the mouseway. They could still hear Milton's angry whining and wailing below them. The realization that they were safe flooded over them. Relief surged through the group, and they laughed uproariously.

"Did you see that fat cat move?" Dillon yelled and slapped his knee.

Julian shouted over the roar. "He must have had hot peppers in his milk!"

"Dillon, you wild thing!" Allister gave him a high five. "You were a crazy mouse."

"What about *you*?" Julian said to Allister. "Dancing on his head!"

Allister repeated the fast stepping he had done on Milton's head to delight the junior he-mice. He had won. He had been last to leave the playing field, and everyone knew it.

"Willy! Bob!" Allister remembered, "You were pinned! Are you all right?"

Personal body surveys revealed the two captives had only sustained minor puncture wounds. The bleeding was stopped with simple pressure and a twist of the surrounding fur.

Then Allister inspected the one-inch scratch on his own tail. It didn't hurt much. Dillon and Julian were unscathed.

As they limped home, methodical Willy remembered Charlie. "Hey! What happened to Charlie?" Dumbfounded that they had overlooked him, the boys blinked stupidly at each other.

Julian spoke up, "He was the first to run. He's probably safely in his nest by now."

Allister was surprised to find his pride at winning the game had faded. And the knowledge that Charlie had failed held no pleasure for Allister.

A small cough came from a recess in the mouseway. All the young he-mice turned to see Charlie skulking toward them. His head was dropped in shame now. "I'm sorry," he said.

Allister stepped up to Charlie and put his arm around him. "It doesn't matter, Charlie. It's a stupid game and doesn't mean a thing." Allister realized the truth in these words as he spoke them.

Reluctantly, the group broke up as they went their separate ways. Allister's tail started to burn as he turned up the mouseway that led toward the kitchen.

His pace slowed a bit as he thought about explaining his war wound to his family, but he walked on, deeply grateful to be going home.

Home. Hey, what's that on the doorway? thought Allister. A small piece of the newspaper-carpet was pinned to the entrance of the family mouse hole with a splinter of wood.

"Found Out!" was the entire note. Fear beat in Allister's ears. His nose wrinkled from the scent of recent panic. Carefully, peeking into the opening, Allister beheld a devastating sight.

∼ 3 ∼

The Spencer home was in shambles. Matchbox drawers lay haphazard with contents scattered everywhere. His own lint bed was strewn randomly around the room. What had happened? His heart stopped when he saw something red in his baby brothers' bedding.

"The Quints!" he called. Frantically, he pawed through the straw shavings, frightened of what he might find. Allister uncovered his mother's red scarf. He looked a little longer and then breathed deeply, satisfied that none of the tiny babies had been hurt or abandoned.

Allister felt so alone. He hunched in a corner wondering what to do. What could the note mean? Who found them out? Allister tied his mother's scarf on his wounded tail. Just as he cinched the last loop, the slam of the cafeteria door vibrated the walls.

"We found a nest of 'em in this here cupboard," a man's deep voice said. Two sets of boots stomped toward their home. Allister froze with horrible anticipation. The cupboard door flew open, and the floor of the cupboard pulled up, exposing Allister.

"Aawk!" one man cried. He almost dropped the floor board, but the second man caught it.

"Get the critter!" he yelled. The first

man stepped high intending to crush Allister with his boot. But in his excitement, his foot came down on his partner's hand, smashing it between his boot and the floorboard's edge.

"Ya-ha-ha-hoo!" the man's scream followed Allister down the mouseway.

Allister ran, what in the mouse community is known as, a "switch." This was a path back and forth through the mouseways. It took three times longer to get to a destination because one repeatedly doubled back on oneself. But when a mouse wanted to be sure of not being caught, this strategy confused trackers.

Of course, the men were much too large to follow Allister through the mouseways, but he obediently followed the drill his father had taught him.

Allister came upon "Cat's Crossing."

This was a particularly tricky crossing of mouseways that came together in a central place that was shaped rather like a cat, with five runways forming the tail and four legs. There was even an abandoned mouseway that formed a small cave for the head.

As Allister ran from the "tail" mouseway down the first "leg," he thought he heard something. He stopped. Only the men's voices echoed softly in the distance. I guess my animal instincts are playing tricks on me, he thought. Two more times through Cat's Crossing and I'll head for Lannie's Loop. Allister scampered through the ways and doubled back. As he entered Cat's Crossing for the second time his ears perked again.

"Allister!" a coarse whisper called. Allister stopped short. He willed his heart to stop beating in his ears, but the trill continued.

"Who's there?" he whispered back into the cavernous blackness of Cat's Crossing.

"Over here," the answer floated from the head end of the cavern.

Allister slid closer, hoping beyond hope. Finally, a familiar scent was caught.

"Dad!" Allister yelled. He ran to his father and threw paws around Duke's neck, hugging him wildly. Duke seemed to ease into Allister's joy.

"OK, OK," Duke finally said. "The Creator has extended our time together again, but the crisis is far from over. There will be other times for joy."

Allister responded quickly. "Dad, where is the family?"

"The Whittier family invited us to stay with them in the teacher's lounge until we can find something else. I was waiting for you, since you hadn't returned from your evening raid for food before we had to leave."

Father sniffed suspiciously at Mom's scarf on Allister's tail. "I figured you'd come through Cat's Crossing sometime. Did you have any trouble?"

"No," lied Allister. He was happy to be on the move towards the teacher's lounge. "But what happened?" he asked.

"The custodian found a few doops on the floor of the cafeteria," Duke said.

Allister's ears burned red. "It wasn't me! It was probably those O'Shea brats!"

"There's no point in looking for blame now," Father spoke firmly. "We all know that mouse droppings are like a red flag to humans. It's as much the mouse parents' fault for not following their young with a doop scoop. The point is that our home was found out. It will be cleaned out, sanitized, and booby-trapped until man thinks we're gone. It's just not safe."

"I know," Allister sighed. "But the teacher's lounge? I hear the place smells like coffee grounds and old lettuce."

"It's a place to be," Father answered.

"There's not much food there," recalled Allister.

"Not compared to our cafeteria, of course," Father admitted, "but we'll make do until the council okays a new spot for us."

Mother was so glad to see Allister that she forgot he was nearly a he-mouse as she kissed him. She closed her eyes in pleasure as she licked his face and ears.

"Mom!" Allister protested, while wriggling away. "I'm fine!"

"I know, dear, I know. Isn't the Creator good?" she cooed and then started. "What's this? My scarf! Oh, Allister, you saved my mother's scarf! I was so sad to think I had dropped it in our rush to escape." Mother slid the scarf off Allister's tail in one long swoop.

"Ya-ouch!" Allister cried. His wound glistened in the morning sun coming through the lounge window.

"Allister! Oh poor, poor mousie! What happened to my boy?" Mother crooned.

"It's nothing, Mom," he said as he flipped his tail behind him.

"*Nothing?*" Mother retorted, rotating Allister in a circle to try to get to his tail.

"I think he's right, Melba," Duke said calmly. "For a junior he-mouse playing Chicken with a cat, I'd say he came out amazingly well."

Mother stopped spinning Allister who was blinking in an effort to make the room stop spinning.

"Is this true, Allister?" Mother asked softly. "Did you deliberately disobey your father?"

"Well, I learned something," he mumbled.

It truly hurt Allister to see the sadness in his mother's face, but it hurt him more to feel his father's firm hand of discipline on the bottom of Allister's repentance. Allister walked stiffly, his rump smarting, to the far corner of the lounge where his siblings were huddled.

"Have a seat?" Elizabeth offered with

a grin. Allister ignored her. He nuzzled the baby quints and curled around them for his day's sleep, grateful to be with his family— even Elizabeth.

∽ 4 ∽

It was only noon when his father woke him. "I want you to come with me to a council meeting." His father placed a piece of hard corn in Allister's sleeping paw.

He wanted to complain of his throbbing tail and go back to sleep, but his father's simple statement was flashing in his mind like lightning. Allister nodded his agreement as his sharp teeth nibbled at the germ end of the kernel.

The council. Wow, thought Allister. He realized the importance of even being allowed within earshot of such a meeting.

Father combed Allister's topknot with his claw as he spoke. "You are not to talk, or even look in the eyes of the council judges. You and Elizabeth won't be called as witnesses because you are not of age, but you and your siblings are allowed to be present as children of the stricken family. Time is of the essence since the community needs to draw up a plan of response. "

The council meeting was held under the bunk bed in the nurse's office. The lights were dimmed, even when a sick human child was bedded there. Elizabeth, his mother, and he sat on the sidelines as the six judges filed in and took their places in the Semi-Circle of Wisdom.

Allister's father was the third judge to

enter, right after Charlie's father. It steamed Allister that Charlie's father had been appointed to the council only a week after they arrived at McAllister School. Finally, Senior Judge Jonathan MacDougall, Dillon's father, came into the room.

"Explain to me again how mankind found you out," Charlie's father asked after they were all seated. Allister squirmed. His father explained the unfortunate discovery in the cafeteria that gave away their family's location.

William Willows, Willy's dad, a zealous little mouse, offered to shape paper cones for each family to hang by the entrance to their holes so that they would be more responsible.

An ordinance had been drawn up by another judge, Samuel P. Rutherford, who grandly proposed a new law, reading it as loudly as he safely could under the sickroom bed. It sounded very fine, and of course, avoided the word "doop" at all costs.

Afterwards, Senior Judge Jonathan McDougall cleared his throat, "It's a good deal of words you've put together, Sam. And no small amount of time it took you, I'm sure. Thank you."

"Shall we vote to pass it then?" Charlie's dad asked.

"I can't say that I think our community needs another law about a common sense issue that every mouse parent knows." Judge McDougall said. "I suggest this family's story be told around each table tonight. That seems like warning enough." A silent agreement circled the room. Judge Jonathan went on, "The important issue now is finding the Spencer family a home. What is available?"

Charlie's dad suggested, "What about

the third grade room? No one lives there."

An embarrassed still came over the Semi-Circle. Allister turned his head and mouthed the words, "Well, roll my eyeballs."

Finally, Allister's father spoke. "There's a moratorium on the third grade room," he said. "We lost the entire Petree family there two months ago. It was a trap."

"Oh, I'm sorry," he apologized. "I totally forgot."

"May I repeat my offer to split the teacher's lounge?" Mr. Whittier said.

"But the rule is 'One family to a room,'" Samuel P. Rutherford bellowed impatiently.

"It could be a hardship on you, brother," Duke reminded Mr. Whittier.

"Can't some consideration be given as to the size of our family? With just my daughter and me there, we would welcome the Spencer family."

"I would be willing to take 'Squatter's Rights and Responsibilities,'" Duke said. A respectful silence followed. Allister's mouth fell open. He was about to protest when Melba tapped him on the shoulder and frowned her disapproval.

Squatter Rights and Responsibilities, or SR&R, as it was sometimes called, would put the Spencer family in a position of servitude to the Whittier family.

"We will be slaves!" Allister wanted to shout to his dad, but he remained silent. He realized his father knew full well that Mr. Whittier would have ultimate say in decisions, and the Spencer family would have to gather food for the Whittiers—like slaves.

Allister thought of the humiliation he would know as the only young he-mouse to be a slave. "All this in exchange for living in a place that stinks and has no food!" thought Allister. He could not believe his ears.

Judge Jonathan spoke. "Considering the situation of each family, I believe it's a good thing. If Mr. Whittier agrees, we'll take a vote."

So, Allister's family entered the council in honor, but left as the lowest ranking family in the community. Melba, Elizabeth, and Allister were excused from the council meeting at this point.

Allister was glad for the darkness of the mouseway to hide his shame. He tried not to think of what it would be like to live life as a slave. Would Charlie laugh when he heard he was a servant to Old Man Whittier?

Allister slowed as he came upon his new mouse home—the avocado green couch in the teacher's lounge. The inside of the couch was quiet except for the busy sound of cleaning. It must be *Princess* Alanna, he thought spitefully.

Allister hadn't seen Alanna for months. She had been spending all of her spare time working for a mouse family in the school office cupboard, in exchange for food. Allister threw open the black fabric over the back of the couch. Alanna didn't look up. She was busily preparing enough food for an army. Her very efficiency irritated him.

"So, who are you...Speedy Gonzalez?" Allister taunted her.

Alanna froze. She turned to face Allister and began to blush. She had thick, fluffy fur the color of antique lace, but it couldn't hide the flush that rose from her thin cheeks to her large, black eyes. Even her nose and ears reddened.

"I...um, well, I didn't...hear, uh. What?" She was pulling on her apron's hem as she spoke.

Allister felt like a brat. "I'm sorry," he said. "I didn't mean to startle you. Let me help."

All mice are born with the instinct to know how to clean a nest. This primary directive moved the two in their actions. They worked quickly. Neither of them spoke, but Allister felt bonded in one spirit in a way he had never known. On occasion Alanna's dainty claw would drag lightly over Allister's paw, or their eyes would lock as they stood at either end of the handkerchief they were folding. But Allister had to guess if Alanna was feeling the same special connection.

Suddenly she stopped. "What?" asked Allister, confused.

"We're finished," Alanna answered.

"Allister!" His mother's voice broke their magic moment. "Allister, are you here?" As she entered she carried a quint on each hip and pulled a third by the tail as it scrambled to get away.

Elizabeth followed with the other two. She scolded Allister, "We hurried the best we could and looked for you at every turn, hoping you'd help carry a quint."

Melba plopped the quints down in a corner, "Yes, Allister, you should have helped with the quints. They are getting so big! Well, anyway, you made it back."

Allister crouched in an opposite

corner.

"Alanna," Mother spoke in surprise, "you sure do know how to keep a clean nest. This place is spotless!"

"Allister helped…" She stopped when she saw Allister shake his head behind his mother's back.

"Allister?" Mother was amazed. "Well, I'll be! My good little mousie!" She turned around to look at Allister, but he was heading up a board of the couch's frame to a sleeping loft.

In the loft, Allister licked his tail one more time and then wound himself down into his straw bed. Sleep tried to cover him at once, but his mind kept seeing those big, black eyes.

∽ 5 ∾

Life in the lounge wasn't luxurious, but Allister found living in the same home as Alanna—well—lovely, although he never would have admitted it. Allister decided that serving the Whittiers was not so bad after all. October flew by, and suddenly it was time for the school harvest party.

Allister's nightly runs for food had become routine with the goal to finish and get home. But today, Allister was unusually anxious to get started. He could not find a comfortable place to sit as he waited for McAllister Elementary School to be out, so he paced the floor and mumbled.

"Settle down," Mom chided. "You're making everyone nervous."

Two of the quints, Que and Quinn, started chewing on each others' ears as if to prove their mother's statement.

"Stop that, boys!" she scolded. "You'll put nicks in your ears. And Allister, why do you have two bags? You won't be able to carry them both if they are loaded, will you?"

Allister answered impatiently. "I am not a micette any more, Mother. All he-mice carry extra bags."

His mother nodded with a sad look on her face, which irritated Allister all the more. "Why don't you let me go early?" he pleaded. "All the teachers are in class, and I promise to wait in the mouseway until the last man is gone."

"No, Allister," his mother refused again. "You know the council agreed only grown-mice could go out collecting food today before the going home bell. The men's children will be crazy with excitement because of the parties."

"But Mother, I *am* grown—or almost."

Melba knew that there was truth in this statement. "OK. You can go to Cat's Crossing to wait for the last bell." Her good-bye warnings swirled in the tornado Allister created as he shot out the door.

Cat's Crossing was empty when Allister got there, but he smelled many mixed scents of neighboring mice that had recently passed through on their way to the hunt.

Then he heard, "Allister." He turned to see Julian approaching from a leg of Cat's

Crossing. "What are you doing out of your nest, Buddy? You're still a junior, aren't you?" Julian had gone through the he-mouse rite of passage just last week. He didn't like Allister being granted any special privileges before his time.

Allister stumbled around in his mind. What should he say to Julian? Would he be in trouble with the council for being out early? Allister thought of his mother's reluctant agreement to let him go. "My mother told me I *had* to come here," he said. This was almost true.

Julian tilted his head, looking quizzically at Allister. "Is that right?"

"Yes," Allister blurted, "She asked me to take an extra bag to my father." Allister held up one of his bags.

"Really?"

Allister's tongue was frozen in his

mouth. He couldn't answer so he nodded his head.

Julian rubbed the short whiskers that were newly growing from his chin. He thought a second and then spoke softly, "I don't know why you're lying to me."

"Lying!" Allister bristled. "I'm not lying. My mother agreed that I could leave early if I came here to wait for the bell."

Julian crossed his arms. "That's a little different than what you first said; that your mother told you that you *had to* come here— to bring your dad an extra bag?"

Just then the going home bell vibrated through the building.

Rats! thought Allister. The good stuff will be gone before I get there. "Look, Julian, nobody made you hall monitor. I've gotta go gather food and stuff." He pushed past Julian who stepped firmly on Allister's tail.

Allister tried to run forward but his tail was nailed to the spot, and it caused him to jolt backwards and land on his bottom at Julian's feet.

The look in Julian's eyes scared Allister. Julian's glare softened into a plea for Allister to listen as Julian spoke. "Allister. Don't do this. You are called to so much more. Don't you know that?"

Allister sat quietly and finally listened.

Julian spoke softly to him. "The Creator has a special calling for you. You need to walk in the truth of the Light—not in lies and the half-truths of the world. He can't use you if you aren't straight up."

Allister blinked at Julian. What did he mean? Could it be true that the Creator had a special plan just for him? And how would Julian know that? But Allister could not ask any questions. Instead, he bowed his head and said, "I'm sorry, Julian. I don't know why I lied. Will you forgive me? I really am sorry."

"Look at me," Julian said as he stepped off of Allister's tail. "I love you, Bud. Been watching you since you were born. You're something special, Allister. Do what's right, OK?"

Allister saw something in Julian he had never seen before. It was the same confidence that had always radiated from Julian, but this time his confidence was about Allister. He was speechless, yet again.

Then Julian turned and jetted off down a leg of the intersection, holding his gathering bag in his mouth.

Food! The thought exploded Allister's muscles into action. He had never moved so quickly through the walls of the old school. Seconds later, he peeped through a crack in the baseboard of the third grade room.

The students were filing out of the outside door, going to be picked up by their parents. It slammed behind the last one with a Ka-bang!

"Party time!" Allister squeaked. He scurried over a jump rope, a pencil, and a book that had a picture on the front of a mouse riding a motorcycle. This caused Allister to pause and laugh. "What ridiculous imaginations these humans have!"

Allister looked up and then—he saw it. It was easily four times bigger than he was. What was it? Allister wasn't sure, but he thought it was an entire popcorn ball! Caramel, he decided as he took a lick of the brown, sticky stuff globbed on the popped corn and holding it together.

Allister knew there was no time to waste. The teacher would be back from seeing the kids off in fifteen minutes, or less.

If he took the time to break the ball down he might only be able to move a fourth of it to the mouseway before the teacher returned. But, Allister reasoned, *if I can get this out the hallway door and down the hall to the broom closet, I can hide it there until I break up the entire thing.*

He was absolutely giddy with his plan. It would feed his family and the Whittiers for a week, maybe two. He would be a hero. No, he rethought that idea. *I didn't really do so well when I tried to outdo everyone last time. No, I will just be a grateful mouse if the plan works.*

The ball rolled easily over the carpet of the classroom. The door to the inside hall was ajar sufficiently to get the ball through. At the crack, Allister peeked to one side and then the other. The coast was clear.

However, the caramel stuck on the

hardwood floor of the hall. His hind claws scratched the floor as he pumped his legs, trying to move the weight of the popcorn ball. His front paws were sticky from rolling the ball across the classroom, but he didn't mind as the syrup seemed to bind his paws to the corn as he shoved.

The ball took static jumps forward, causing Allister to realize his dilemma. He couldn't move the ball, but he must! If he took much longer he would surely be spotted. Allister ran a few tight circles around the ball trying to think of a way out. He approached the monster again. This time he shoved against it with all—his—might! Nothing.

Just when all seemed hopeless, the outside door of the room flew open and a third grade girl child tumbled into the room.

"J-j-j-just a minute," she yelled behind her. The girl child flew to the desk in the corner where Allister had found the popcorn ball. She bent to her hands and knees to look on the floor. "I know I must have dropped it by my desk," she said out loud.

Up until now, Allister was a little concerned that he was in what is called "wide spaces" in the mouse community, meaning he was fully visible.

But this is not as dangerous as a human might expect, since a mouse is rarely noticed huddled on the edge of a room—unless the mouse moves. Allister had been trained in the technique of standing perfectly still until the danger was over since his mousette days of Freeze Tag. But now Allister's confidence in his being invisible was melting as he began to realize that the girl was looking for *his* popcorn ball. Yikes!

Even more frightening was the realization that in his last mighty push, he had shoved his paws deep into the caramel mass, and now, he was glued to it!

"There you are." The girl child chided the popcorn ball as she approached the doorway. Her footsteps came closer and closer.

Allister closed his eyes tightly, bracing for the pain of the girl crushing him when she saw him. He tensed and shuddered but the blow did not come. At last, when he could bear it no longer, he screamed, "CHEE! CHEE! CHEE-KOI!"

Silence followed.

Allister would have held the pose until death fell, but now the suspense was killing him. He peeked open one eye, only to see a large human eye gazing at him. He clamped his eyes shut again and waited.

"Caramel is my favorite, too," the girl child laughed. "What should I do with you?"

Allister opened both eyes now and relaxed his shoulders.

"What's your name, mousie?" she inquired.

"Allister—and I'm not a *'mousie.'*" He answered before he remembered the ordinance that forbids mice from ever talking to man.

The girl child did not seem to think it odd that Allister spoke. More, she replied thoughtfully, "That's a good name. My name is Bree. Well, Allister," she said, "we need to get you, and your meal, to safety."

Without further discussion, Bree picked up the popcorn ball in one hand, with Allister still firmly attached to it, and carefully picked up Allister with the thumb and forefinger of the other.

Allister hated her touch. Her smell could permeate his spaces for weeks! Where was she taking him? Bree walked into the hall, opened the broom closet door, and set him and the popcorn ball in the back corner behind an empty bucket where he wouldn't be found.

"I've got to go now. My mom's waiting. I hope you'll be OK." She paused a minute and then smiled. "You'll be fine. Nice meeting you, Mr. Allister. Bye." She waved and shut the door. Allister could not believe his luck—or was it luck?

6

As soon as Bree closed the closet door, Allister began chewing at the caramel around his paws. Who would find him next in this dangerous position—stuck to a popcorn ball? Holy Mackerel! He had to get moving.

As he worked, a sober gratitude came over him. Julian was right. The Creator had seen fit to send help. The Creator was saving him out. But for what?

Mice voices sounded in the distance.

"Where'd he go?"

"I think he's in here!"

Allister recognized the voices as those of Charlie and Dillon just before the two mice teens squeezed under the door.

"Wow!" exclaimed Charlie. "We thought you were a goner. How did you talk her into putting you in here?" Charlie bit a big hunk of caramel near Allister's wrist.

"I didn't," answered Allister, "it was her idea."

"Sure," said Dillon, his fists on his hips, "next you'll be telling us that you didn't talk to her at all. Don't lie about it, Allister. We heard you tell her your name."

Allister ignored his accuser and kept chewing around his entrapped paws. Soon, he was free.

Charlie looked disappointed to have the job done and licked his lips as he spoke.

"Cool down, Dillon. We should be grateful Allister's safe, and that we have all this food to share."

"Share?" said Dillon. "I found it first! If it hadn't been for Allister, we would have had the entire thing broken up and in the mouseway before that girl child ever got back!"

Allister was angry now. "I could have been killed for this. I found it first, and that gives me 'First Found Rights.'"

Charlie looked apologetic and said, "Actually, Dillon's right, Allister. He spotted the ball first from the south wall. He left the F.F.R. scent, just like we're supposed to, and came to get me to help."

"That's right!" cried Dillon. "And as far as I can see, there's no reason the most prominent family in the town should have to give up the best find of the night to a 'slave' mouse."

Allister's jaw dropped.

Dillon had his nose so far in the air that he didn't notice his father's arrival behind him.

"That's funny," Judge McDougall said. "I can't think of a better reason you should give the popcorn ball to Allister."

The voice startled Dillon who jumped straight up, turned, and landed facing his father.

"Dad!" Dillon cried. "I marked 'First Found Rights.' And besides, he broke the law by talking to man and then lied about not doing it." Dillon was out for blood.

"No. No, I didn't lie to you, Dillon. I didn't say anything." Allister did not want to be accused of being a liar again, and this time, he was not.

"Dillon," Charlie spoke up, "being so

honest, I suppose you wouldn't mind if I reported seeing you leave the doop in the kitchen that put the Spencer family out of a home?"

Dillon's ears turned purple. "I didn't do that," he sputtered. He looked at his father and quivered. "I didn't mean to!" he yelled.

The three other mice stared at him. Dillon turned to Allister, pleading, "If I had known, Allister, I swear I would have been more careful."

Allister continued to stare at Dillon in disbelief.

Judge McDougall sighed. "What do you think, Allister? Should Dillon be punished for dropping the fatal doop?"

Allister spoke, "At first, it was pretty tough to be slaves. But then I saw that when we served, the Creator gave us lots of good things that we never could have imagined." He turned to Dillon and clapped his paw on Dillon's shoulder, "I know what it's like to do something you are sorry about. You may have done that on purpose, or not, but the Creator used it for good. I forgive you, Dillon."

"Well, Dillon," Judge McDougall said, "seems like you've got the chance to right a wrong. Since the food is yours, you have the privilege of giving it to Allister."

Dillon was crushed and started to cry. "I'm sorry, Allister. I'm sorry, Dad. I didn't know what would happen to the Spencer family, honest." Dillon stopped crying and wiped his nose on his scarf. The mice gave Dillon a chance to compose himself. "Of course, you can have the popcorn ball, Allister. If it wasn't for me, you'd still have your home."

"I appreciate the offer, but it's going to be a struggle to move this. How about if we each take a fourth to our homes; one fourth to ours, one fourth to Charlie's, and two fourths to yours? What do you think, Judge McDougall?"

"No, Allister," Dillon interrupted. "Dad was right. I'll take my fourth to your home with the Whittiers."

"You can have my part as well," answered Judge McDougall.

Charlie looked nervous. He did not want to give up his portion and leave his family hungry.

"It's OK, Charlie," Allister assured him. "We couldn't possibly eat it all."

"If you're sure..." asked Charlie.

"Enjoy it," Allister said. It felt good to pay back Charlie for his support.

The mouseways were traffic jams of

sweet treats on the way back to the teachers' lounge. Duke and Melba were so happy to see the three big pieces of popcorn ball that they begged Dillon and his family to come to dinner—after they had asked their master, Mr. Whittier, of course.

A short time later the McDougalls arrived. Maria McDougall squeezed through the couch opening first with two micettes on each hip.

"Hola! Hola! Como estas frijole?" Maria's face held a permanent smile, but her eyes held the key to their meaning. Now her eyes were smiling. She chirped, "That means, 'Hello! Hello! How y'all *bean*?'" Her laughter sounded like merry bells.

Maria, Dillon's mother, had arrived in Trinity a few years back in a crate of Mexican grown tomatoes, only to sweep Dillon's father off his paws.

Judge McDougall followed behind his wife, smiling fondly at her joke, even though he had heard it a million times. He carried a fresh find of wheat crackers and cheese crumbs for which the quints began to jump instinctively.

"Sit down, quints!" Melba scolded. "Where's Dillon?" she asked holding her paw on the top of Quaid's head, as if to keep him from rising into the air.

"He's coming," Maria said. "I think he may be making sure his top knot is fluffed for a couple of ladies I know." She smiled coquettishly, winking at Alanna and Elizabeth.

At sleep time, Allister curled in his bed of straw. He thought about how easily he had fallen into lying to Julian. The thought made his ears burn in shame.

But what had Julian said to him about the Creator? That He had a plan for Allister? When Julian spoke those words, Allister knew they were true. Maybe truer than any other words he had ever heard.

But what did they mean? Allister didn't know. Something about the idea frightened him—and thrilled him at the same time. He decided he would not think about it and slipped into dreamland.

November froze solid, into a whipper-snapping cold. Allister shivered as he came home from the hunt to the dinner table. He was unusually tired and ready for bed. As he sat down, he noticed Mr. Whittier was not in his normal seat at the head of the table.

"Where's your father, Alanna?" Allister asked.

Her face clouded a bit. "He was very tired and not hungry, so he decided to take tea in bed."

Elizabeth sat beside Allister with a quint on each knee. She handed one to Allister as she spoke. "You know what today is, don't you, Allister?"

"Uh…," he hedged.

"Surprise!" yelled Mother as she popped a large marshmallow out from under a cap of a can of hair spray. On top of the marshmallow, Mother had carefully nibbled the words, "Happy Birthday."

Allister blinked, surprised and confused. Birthdays weren't something mice usually celebrated, but Mother was an anthropologist of a sort. She loved studying men. And since she loved parties, she especially loved studying their holidays.

"This means you are both one year old," Mother said proudly.

"Uh-huh," Allister politely responded,

but he really wanted to ask, "So what?"

Elizabeth smiled at her mother as she waited.

"A first birthday is very special in human families. Of course, since we mice generally live only three or four years…"

"Unless the good Creator calls us home first," Father interrupted.

"Yes, of course," agreed Mother. "Well, that means that we may only have a few birthdays. So, Happy Birthday, dears!" She kissed them both on top of their heads.

Duke watched patiently and then spoke, "This *is* a turning point for you two," Father added. "It's time for you to begin learning your adult roles. Even though we mice are born with instinctual knowledge, a well-rounded mouse schools in special studies. I've gotten permission from the Semi-Circle of Wisdom for the two of you and Alanna to attend classes in the third grade room. Your father agrees, Alanna."

"School?" Allister protested. "We know everything we need to know."

Allister was grouchy when Father woke him three hours later to start classes. He might have complained except he remembered that at least Alanna was going with him.

Just before Lannie's Loop, Elizabeth, Allister, and Alanna heard a voice behind them. "Allister! Wait up!" It was Charlie.

"Hey, Charlie," Allister said. "What are you up to?"

"I'm going to school—the third grade class—with you."

"Cool! Dad didn't tell us that." Allister gave Charlie a high-five paw slap.

Duke had given specific instructions

about viewing the class. They were to sit behind the heater duct in the side wall of the class. If they sat to the back of the duct, Father was sure they couldn't be seen.

All four mice-teens had kernels tucked into their cheeks to nibble as they learned. Looking through the grid of the heater duct, the four of them could see past several of the man children's legs to the teacher at the front of the class.

"Today we are going to study our country's first official holiday. Who can guess what that is?" Miss Phillips asked.

A small boy in the front shot up his hand with so much fervor that he almost knocked his glasses off. His hand strained frantically in the air.

"Yes, Peter?" She called on him, wanting to put him out of his misery.

Then, he looked blank, as if he were

trying to remember the question. "Ah— birthdays?"

Elizabeth's ears perked with interest.

The teacher smiled. "Well, I don't actually know if birthdays were celebrated then. I mean holidays that everyone in the country celebrates at the same time."

Half the class had their hands up now, looking ever so much like a catch of flopping fish.

"Yes, Audrey?" The teacher pointed to a prim-looking, blond girl in the middle of the room.

"I believe the first holiday would be Christmas," she spoke carefully.

"That's a good guess," the teacher answered. "But I was asking about the first holiday in our country. I believe the first holiday celebrated was Thanksgiving. It was a first feast, a big food party."

Ahs and ums filled the little room. Allister and Charlie leaned forward, hoping to hear something about access to food.

"Does anyone know what the people were called who celebrated the first Thanksgiving?" Miss Phillips asked.

"Injuns!"

"Pilgrims!"

"Mayflowers!"

"We need to raise our hands. Some of you are right. We call these early settlers from England 'Pilgrims', because they were in a new land." She pointed to a map. "After first settling in Holland for a time, they came over the Atlantic Ocean on a ship called the Mayflower. Who knows when they got here? Remember—hands."

No one stirred at all.

She continued, "Well, they landed in what is now Massachusetts in 1620, over

150 years before our country's first birthday. Does anyone know when that was?"

"July 4, 1776!" piped up several children.

"Absolutely right!" Miss Phillips smiled. "So back to the Pilgrims—they got here in November. Why would that be a problem?"

"Because they had nothing," James answered with his hands opened wide and empty.

"That's right, James, or at least they had very little by the time the group had crossed that big ocean. They had used up most of their food and much of what was left was rotten. There were no stores to buy things like food, clothes, or blankets to keep warm. Some Native Americans helped, but it was a very hard time."

Allister felt tense.

"Even with the Native Americans' help, half the Pilgrims died that first winter. In the spring, the Pilgrims planted seeds. So, by summer, they had lots of food for the coming year. How do you think they felt about that?"

"I'd be glad," Sam answered softly.

"I would thank the Native Americans," said Patrick, feeling sure he had the right answer.

"And that's a good thing," Miss Phillips agreed. "But the Pilgrims knew that their real help came from God, their Creator. So they thanked God in three days of prayer. Then they invited the Native Americans to join them in a big feast."

Andrew, a freckled, round-faced boy in the back, raised his hand quietly.

"Yes, Andrew?" Miss Phillips asked.

"Why were those people happy and having a party and stuff, when half of them died?"

"It's hard to understand, Andrew, but the Pilgrims were wise in knowing to be thankful for the good things their Creator gave them, as well as the hard things. You see, He gave them the hard times for their good. They believed that God Himself is good. That was enough."

"I don't understand," Andrew said, shaking his head.

"It's not easy to understand," Miss Phillips said quietly. Just then the bell rang.

8

The four mice teens moved back from the heater vent and plodded home. All of them were ready for their afternoon naps, as they had a full night's work ahead of them.

"I don't get it," confessed Allister. "I don't understand life."

"Really, Allister, you're so dense," Elizabeth began. "It's simple. The Creator made mice and gave us good things and the will, strength, and instinct to do right. So,

81

everything is good."

"I think it's amazing when men who do evil, also choose to do right," Alanna countered.

"Well, there is truth in what you both said," waffled Charlie.

"Actually, Elizabeth's often wrong but never in doubt," Allister spiked. Elizabeth wrinkled her nose at him.

Charlie spoke up, "Seriously, Allister, I think the teacher's lesson in the story is that many hard things as well as good things come people's way, but all are in the Creator's plan. Those Pilgrim people were thanking the Creator, not just for good times, but for being their God. My father says it's called trusting the Creator."

Silence followed as the four mice pondered that idea.

Allister said, "That's probably hard for

men. They seem to think that they are gods."

Charlie turned off at Cat's Crossing and the three others carefully made their way to the couch in the teacher's lounge. A mouse was crying softly.

"It's Mother!" said Elizabeth.

As they entered the main room Father and Mother were huddled together. The quints were all sleeping in the corner. Then Alanna saw the problem. A paper cloth lay draped over a form on a soft bed of straw.

"Papa! He's…" Alanna's voice caught in her throat.

Melba came forward and wrapped Alanna in her arms. "It just happened. He came out of his nest and knew he was going. He asked us to let you choose a home and then closed his eyes as if he were going to sleep. His last thoughts were of you."

Alanna turned away from Melba and

caught Allister. He held her kindly as she cried her eyes dry on his shoulder. Then she went to her nest for a long and sorrowful sleep.

The next morning Alanna awoke just in time for breakfast. She could not believe she had slept through the whole night. At the breakfast table everyone seemed to be uncomfortable, wondering how to talk to her.

"Well," started Alanna. "I've been thinking about my father's last words."

Elizabeth and Melba started to cry. "You could stay with us as our daughter," Father offered, and Mother nodded with enthusiasm.

"Thank you," Alanna responded. "I really do appreciate all you have done for me and my father. Papa used to tell me every night how he thanked the Creator for sending you to care for us. He was just too old to go out and find dinner every night— and then for you to treat him as master... well, you all have been just wonderful." She looked around the table, and then her dark black eyes rested on Allister as she continued in a firm and steady voice, "But, I've decided to go live with the Lindstroms. You see..."

Allister's world burst like a balloon. He hardly heard Alanna's explanation that Charlie's mother, Nanette, was expecting a new litter of micettes any day.

"What?" Allister was shocked.

Alanna blushed. "Yes, and Mrs. Lindstrom is so refined, I'm not sure she is up to another litter. In Paris very few mice ever had more than one litter. When she was trapped in that designer clothing shipment and shipped to Chicago... well, I think she might need some help with things, not ever having a daughter."

Allister imagined Charlie's handsome face snickering at Alanna choosing him.

Duke's voice broke into Allister's nightmare. "Alanna, I'm happy to see you are thinking about others in your time of distress. It's a good thing to do. Elizabeth, help Alanna move her things today."

And so it was over—the months of happy camaraderie that Allister had shared with Alanna. It had all been a dream. But why did this reality of her leaving seem like the dream? Allister floated through the next few weeks in this fog until one afternoon he woke with a start.

The couch seemed to be in the middle of an earthquake. Mother squealed at the family to help find the micettes who had been thrown from their bed like dust balls being swept across a floor. As they were being gathered, the home continued to pitch and sway.

"Allister," Duke called as he caught another dust-bunny mouse rolling past, "find out what's happening out there!"

Allister handed the tail of the mousette he was holding to Elizabeth and ran to the chewed corner of the couch where they normally entered. He hung upside down out the hole. The buildings across the street from McAllister School were jumping before his eyes. Allister thought the whole world was jumping.

"Throw it in duh back, and I'll drive," one man yelled towards the couch.

"This thing weighs a ton!" another man complained.

"Yeah, UFF-DAH! They don't make 'em like 'dis anymore," his companion agreed.

Allister ran to his father. "Dad!" he yelled, "the couch is being moved from the school!"

"Abandon couch!" Dad yelled. The mouse family grabbed only the essentials and jumped out of the truck.

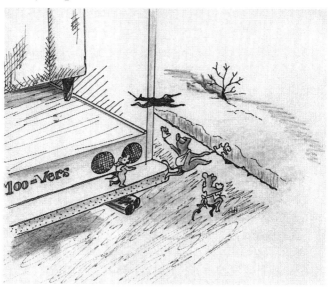

They landed in a muddy snow drift just before the moving men slammed the back door and climbed in the cab. Exhaust from the truck blew black soot on the family and the wheels sprayed slush over them as the truck rattled out of the school driveway.

And the Spencers were homeless again.

Pilgrims, challenged to trust the Creator.

～ 9 ～

There was no doubt about it—this was a gray day. A clammy mist smothered the horizon of dirty snow; a perfect day for being homeless.

Of course, it could have been tragic for the baby quints if the family had been ousted from their home earlier, while their little bodies were bare. But now, as the chilly wind puffed with enthusiasm, the micettes' downy fur only fluffed thicker.

"It's lucky we found this man-child's glove," Melba snapped as she chewed the palm of the glove open and gnawed the yarn edges back to its woolly-sheep state. She began to carefully stuff a quint into each finger of the glove. The babies just fit and looked for all the world like plump little sausages with black noses. Duke had a half smile on his face as he watched Mother in action.

"The glove is the Creator's provision, Melba," he assured her softly. Duke left quietly to hunt for food and a place to stay.

Allister was over his anger at losing Alanna to Charlie, or even losing his family's home for the second time. In fact, he felt rather like his life was over as he curled around the trunk of the bush under which they were hiding.

Elizabeth, began to sniff.

"Please, dear," Mother said, "blow your nose."

Allister thought of several snide remarks to make about Elizabeth's sniffing, but his damp spirit clamped his jaw shut. He inwardly moaned and tightened his curl into a miserable little ball.

"Ah-ah-ah....choo!" Elizabeth sneezed and dabbed her eyes dramatically.

"Oh dear. My poor Lizzie! Oh dear!" Mother worried. "We need to find a place to take you before it snows again, and before the C-A-T comes out." She spelled the word, not wanting to frighten the babies.

"Oh, I'm OK, Mom," Elizabeth said. "That's not what's depressing me."

"Dad will find us a place before tonight when that malicious Milton comes around," Mother said as she re-stuffed one of the sausage babies. "But if being homeless isn't bothering you, what is?"

Elizabeth looked at the quints who were all staring at her through beady eyes. Mother saw the exchange of glances and asked, "What is it, Lizzie?"

"Well, it's...well, I guess it doesn't matter, but...what about Christmas?" she finally blurted out.

All the babies cried, "Yeah, Cwis-mas!"

So, there it was. The epitome of the somber day—laid out like a raw Christmas goose on the kitchen table. But there was no dressing up this fowl. The truth was, there would be no Christmas.

Now, Christmas wasn't exactly what you would call a tradition in the Spencer family. Allister and Elizabeth were tiny micettes last year at this time. Duke and Melba Spencer had moved to McAllister School's kitchen cupboard before the birth of their quadruplets. Elizabeth was born first. Beth and Liza followed, and then little Allister, who was named after McAllister Elementary School, their bounteous new home.

Duke was secretly afraid Allister was too frail to live, but as Providence would have it, it was Beth and Liza who died shortly after their birth of the flu. Allister thrived.

A month after their birth, Christmas had hit McAllister School like a sleigh full of bells. Similar to the Harvest Party, there had been sweets, but the celebrating lasted longer. It seemed every third day there had been a party in the cafeteria which had meant delectable crumbs for the Spencers. Sometimes whole cookies, pieces of fruit cake, or crackers would be found among the celery sticks, peanuts, pretzels, and other discarded goodies.

Mother had decided it was a form of sharing the human children were taught. Father had been doubtful about that and cited the careless attitude the humans showed by throwing their food through the air. That didn't look like sharing to him—especially when they were all yelling, "Food fight!"

But the Spencers gratefully had stored

sweet delights for months of munching. Elizabeth remembered this well, having a sweet tooth. She had promised the quints a sugar feast called 'Christmas' from the time that they were born. But now what? The glorious glut of Christmas gone?

"Mice don't need Christmas," Mother began, in opposition to her normal interest in human traditions. "You can see what it does to the humans here at school. Why, the second grade class ran wildly down the hall after recess last year, almost crushing one of the Howard's micettes! And why? Just to get back to the classroom for a party! Really! And what about how grouchy the teachers get?"

Realizing their loss, the mice fell into a sober silence as they waited for the next provision of the Creator.

"Melba!" Father's voice came ringing

over the snowy embankment like a boy mouse at play. "Melba, let's go! I found a home!" Father's eyes glistened, which made Allister wonder momentarily if Father had been crying.

But he's too happy to cry, Allister thought as he started packing up their belongings.

"Where are we going?" Elizabeth asked.

"It's a surprise." Father dangled the treat before them.

"Oh, Duke," Mother sighed, "you're such a tease."

They looked like a caravan of nomads wandering over the Saharan snowdrifts with their bundles of household goods on their heads and babies under their arms. Duke and Melba were very grateful to be entering the mouseway to their new home.

Allister was suspicious of the path they were taking. "Say," he called up to Dad. "Isn't there still a moratorium on living in this part of the building?"

Duke stopped ahead. He had been moving so quickly and with such a load that he was huffing and puffing as he spoke. "It's—over. It's been—three months today." He stopped and turned to his family to say, "The mouse community is overcrowded here at the school, so this is an especially wonderful blessing by the Creator."

"Oh, Duke," Mother said. "Can't we go back to the teacher's lounge?" Elizabeth looked eager.

"What's this? To a room that smells of coffee grounds and old lettuce? Only the best for my family!"

Duke pushed each quint to Melba through a tiny opening in the third grade cupboard. Melba lined them up like matched petunias along the back of the cupboard wall.

"I've checked this room pretty thoroughly. There is no scent of rats, and there is a cracker cupboard for hard days. The room is warm and dry, and this cupboard hasn't been opened in three to four months. It should be a perfect place to winter."

∽ 10 ∽

Allister liked the new home in an upper cupboard of the third grade class. After he helped settle the quints for their nap, he peeked through the crack where the cupboard doors met. There was Miss Phillips again.

And that strange Bree girl was intently coloring a picture of a yellow dog. Her crayon looked about worn out when she stopped suddenly and looked straight at Allister—or the door in front of Allister. But he could feel her eyes on him. He told himself it wasn't possible for her to see him. He backed slowly away from the doors and returned to helping set up the house.

Their cupboard smelled as if it had not been opened in months—the perfect home. Forgotten old bottles of paint guarded the front doors. Mother was very happy to see dust on the floors.

Elizabeth and the quints were delighted at Miss Phillips' going home talk to the kids. "I'd like everyone to put one of these notices in their backpacks or bags right now." She was handing out red edged paper to each child. "We're going to have our Christmas Around the World Days next week. Each of you need to complete your class project on a foreign country, bring a treat from that land, and wear a costume. I hope to see some good work because you've had a month to think about what you will do..."

"Did you hear that?" Elizabeth asked the quints. Their little eyes beamed as they nodded their heads in unison. "Tweats ev-wy day!"

"Let's hope these children are as generous with us as the ones in the cafeteria," Mother said.

"Oh, I don't think that will be a problem," Duke assured her. He watched one of the third grade boys nail another in the back of the head with a granola bar when Miss Phillips' back was turned.

Father was right, as usual, so the mice raids were easy pickin's as the family worked together to move the vast number of crumbled goodies to their home in the top cupboard. It was the quint's first time in helping to gather food, and although their little jaws grew weary carrying the loot, their hearts were light with the anticipated feasts ahead.

The week went quickly.

"Good-bye, good-bye. Merry Christmas to you, too!" the teacher was calling from the door. "Have a wonderful vacation!" She slammed the door and leaned against it. "Two weeks," she smiled happily and started straightening up the room. She was obviously in a hurry to get away from the school as she gathered her things and put away books.

"I'm not going to need this since I'm going to Mom's," she said. "I should find a place for this until next year."

The cupboard door flew open. The entire Spencer family was clearly exposed and froze where they stood. Gratefully, the cupboard was above Miss Phillips' eye level. The teacher shoved all the bottles of paint to one side. The Spencers ran behind them, and just in time. A wooden box-like structure slammed against the back wall where they had been standing. The cupboard door shut.

"Deck the halls with boughs of holly, Fa-la-la-la-la-la-la-la-la," sang Miss Phillips as she flipped off the lights and left the room.

Even though the mice knew that she was gone, they could not speak. At last Allister broke the silence. "Whew! That was close."

"No kidding," Elizabeth said, "So much for the 'unused' cupboard."

"Elizabeth," warned Mother, "don't be disrespectful."

It was a real mess to work their way out of the corner. The bottles had been shoved into the neat little piles of food that Mother had been organizing. One of the quints was missing when Mother took count.

"Duke!" Mother cried. "Quincy is missing!"

Duke jumped to the top of the highest bottle and surveyed the cupboard from that height.

"Ah-ha!" he called and jumped to the food piles. He shoved his paw in a hill of cake crumbs up to his elbow and pulled out Quincy by the tail.

Quincy took a deep breath of air. "Wow, what a way to go!" he giggled.

The family spent the night rearranging their stash carefully between the bottles and beside the box. At one point Allister disappeared.

"Dad!" he called. Duke rushed around the edge of the box wall. There was Allister standing rigid against the inside wall of the box, frozen in fear.

In the dark of the cupboard Duke saw Allister's attackers. Six little men stood, knelt, and lay in a jumbled pile inside of the box. The figures were still as night; their expressions, peaceful. They had no scent except dust. This last realization put Duke totally at ease.

"These are statues, Allister," Duke assured him.

"But they are our size," Allister worried.

"They're human's toys. Probably a gift for men's children from Santa Claus. Remember, they talked about that?"

"I don't know," said Allister. "I have a funny feeling about these." But he said nothing more, for when he got closer he noticed that the red paint on the mouths of the statues was spread to the cheeks. He felt foolish for thinking they were real.

Melba and Elizabeth had a great time observing the little men and pointing out to Allister and Duke that one of them was actually a woman. It was Elizabeth who found the baby.

"Oh, look!" she cried. "Here's a baby statue." The baby was wrapped in a tiny soft white cloth. "It's like a doll." Elizabeth sighed longingly.

"It's also sleeping in a perfect bed for the quints!" Mother grabbed the baby man doll and threw it to the floor. She started stripping a fresh straw bed. Soon the quints were curled into five little fuzzy balls—in the Christ child's bed.

There wasn't a need for more food that night, but Allister was restless and could not stay in. He ran through the mouse trails listening carefully to avoid meeting any mouse who might want to chat. He wondered for the hundredth time how Alanna was doing.

Up on the roof he noticed that the moon was the color of Alanna's fur. But it was more than missing Alanna that was bothering him tonight. The air was crisp—no, it was frigid. And the snow on the roof was a dazzling splendor of crystals that sparkled in the night.

Allister looked out over the roof tops of Trinity. Street lights sporadically dotted the neighborhoods like giant fireflies. Many houses glittered with Christmas lights, and a joy permeated the night. But why?

He looked toward the stars which twinkled wildly across the blackness. He thought about his father's comment when they were star gazing, *"Some of the ancients say that on a night like this, a mouse can talk to the Creator who made us."*

Allister realized this was just such a night, and the idea fascinated him. But how could a mouse talk to the Creator? Fear shivered down Allister's back. What would a mouse say to the Creator of everything?

"Allister." A small voice whispered his name making Allister jump. He turned and looked every which way around him, but no one was there. Had it just been the wind?

"Allister." The soft voice swirled around him this time. Allister looked up. Could it be the Creator? Was he in danger? Allister wanted to run.

He turned to go but heard again, louder this time, "Allister." The sound of his name knocked him to his knees this time.

"I'm here!" he heard these words come out of his mouth and wondered where they came from.

"Shine the Light."

Allister waited. He huddled into a ball and wondered what those words meant. He wanted to speak, but his body was shaking so hard he could barely form the words. "What light?"

"The Light. You will shine the Light."

"Wh-wh-what does that mean?" asked Allister.

"You are My mousie. Serve Me." Silence followed, and a warmth flooded through Allister's tiny mouse frame.

Oddly, Allister liked being called a "mousie" by the Creator. He savored the warmth he felt in his little bones, and he knew he never wanted to be or do anything again outside of the Creator's presence.

Allister waited quietly in the silent darkness until he started to go numb. He had to go back in soon. He would return to his parent's home, but he was no longer the same mouse. A smile drifted across his lips. The Creator's mousie, he thought.

~ 11 ~

It was late afternoon when Allister awoke. "Come on," Duke called. "We've got a chore to do."

The quints were jumping up and down in the manger with joy. "We want to come! We want to come!"

"No," Duke smiled. "You be good and help your mother clean the house. Allister and I will be back with a treat when you get up tomorrow."

Allister was amazed. His father had never singled him out for a he-mice task. Did his father know about Allister's new status?

Duke led through the mouseways at a pace that almost lost Allister at a few turns, not that he would have admitted that. Duke stopped to rest on the frame of McAllister Elementary School's front door. Allister sat beside him.

"I need your help."

"What is it?" Allister could hardly believe his ears—Dad, asking *him* for help?

"Do you remember the stories that men's children have been telling this last week?"

"Do you mean the Christmas Around the World stories?"

"Right. Your mother has really enjoyed the stories about the gifts. Ever since then she has been pining for a Christmas gift."

"What kind of gift?" Allister asked.

"I'm not sure, but I think it should be something she has been wanting," Father said thoughtfully. "When we moved into this school, Melba was very taken with the lights across the street." He pointed to a line of stores and buildings on the opposite side of the street from the school. "She liked them so much that she wanted to move into that building."

"Which one?" Allister was confused. He was looking at a neon-signed café; a lighted red, white, and blue-poled barbershop; and a large brick building with colored windows.

"That one," Father said as he pointed at the large one. "Sometimes the lights shine bright and sometimes not. But I thought if I could catch some of the pretty light and bring it to her, it would be the best gift yet!" Duke explained.

Light! Allister thought. Is this the light that the Creator wanted him to bring? Allister was ready. Not that the idea made a lot of sense— gifts, catching light— but if Allister could return to the feeling he felt with the Creator last night, he would do anything.

"Let's go," said Allister.

Crossing the street was no problem because a footbridge for men's children spanned the busy street. The building itself looked as if getting in might pose problems, until Father spotted a small hole in the brick, made in a miscalculation when a sign was hung. They climbed the sign that read, "Christmas Eve Service," and then squeezed through the hole.

Allister's heart was racing as he sniffed the blackness. A faint glow lit the end of the trail as it turned a corner. To the light, he thought. Without making a sound, they tip-clawed to the bend and around it.

Blasts of color assaulted their senses. Blinking madly to focus on the source, the he-mice, young and old, were astonished at their find.

They had emerged from the mouse trail to the corner of a ceiling molding. Across the cavernous hall, fantastic lights were glowing wildly as the sun passed through the stained glass windows of the church. Red, green, yellow, and blue rays of light hit the rows of seats and pale walls at every angle.

Allister was so overwhelmed with the light show that he couldn't speak. Duke managed a controlled, "Ah, yes." After an awesome moment had passed, Allister saw something familiar.

"Dad, look!" He pointed to a window of color that blazed the image of a human woman and child. "It's the baby man!" Allister cried.

"What baby?" Duke asked, truly puzzled.

"The one in the box," Allister declared with certainty.

"Box? I don't understand. I guess that's a picture of a man-child, all right, but what do you mean that it's in a box?"

"Don't you remember? The baby doll Mother threw away." Allister was amazed that his father, who usually knew everything, could not grasp the importance of the connection.

"Who is the baby, and what does it mean?" Father asked.

Suddenly, Allister was aware that he didn't really know. He just knew that somehow the baby was very important to the Creator. "I don't know," Allister confessed.

Duke was not uninterested in Allister's thoughts about this, but time in open spaces is dangerous for mice in unfamiliar places. He felt pressured to get a piece of light and get home.

"Let's talk about this later, Allister. I'm going to get closer to the lights. You stay here and stand guard."

Allister did watch for trouble and even checked his father's progress from time to time. But his brain could think of nothing but the great Light and the baby man. What did it all mean?

Allister's confusion was met by his father's sad face when he returned. "It's no use, Allister. I cannot find a way to take the light with me." Allister noticed the glow was quickly fading from the windows.

"Look, Dad, the lights are leaving." So was Duke's joy. Allister and Duke were both reluctant to leave, and even the hefty apple core they found on the way back did not lift their spirits. But Duke was silently thinking.

~ 12 ~

The next afternoon, all of the mice woke early. Excitement "stirred the fur," as the old mouse saying goes, and the suspense raised everyone's voice by at least a third.

"Every mouse to breakfast!" Mother trilled. The table was a red-backed playing card set on three checker stacks. The card table was surrounded by Lincoln Logs for seats that Mother and Elizabeth lugged to the cupboard. In the center of the table was a pyramid of red and green tissue paper balls. The old apple core had been chewed into sauce and placed into the lid of a green felt pen. The sight fairly jingled the day.

"Merry Christmas!" Elizabeth squeaked.

"May-wy Cwis-mas! May-wy Cwis-mas!" the quints cheered wildly.

The din shook the cupboard.

"Can't a mouse get a decent nibble around here without going deaf?" Duke said seriously, but the family knew he was happy. Everyone took their seats except Mother.

"Now," she cooed, "I have some presents for each of you." Allister shot a side look at Father who watched Melba kindly. "Inside the tissue balls are gifts for you to open," she said, looking as pleased as punch.

"Oh boy! Whoopee! Hoo-way!" the quints repeated every cheer with gusto which Elizabeth had taught. Mother passed the balls to each mouse in the family and then motioned for them to be opened.

Cheese! Wonderful cheese. There were several pieces for each in various states of ripening. What a glad day for the Spencer family.

After a full and luxurious meal, Father shoved his end of the log back from the table. "Thank you, Mother. Dinner was truly great," he said. After the micettes repeated their father's praise he continued, "Now, fluff yourselves, everybody. Get ready for cold weather."

Only Allister suspected the destination of their trip as Father started across the school parking lot. The quints had no trouble keeping up as Father and Mother held a quint's paw in each of their own. Allister and Elizabeth swung Quill, the smallest quint between them. They lifted him over the snow lumps, leaving only tail lines behind.

"Look, Quill, it's a snow snake!" they said in mocking, low-voiced terror while pointing at the wiggly indentations behind them. Quill's eyes grew large with fright.

Mother had been flustered to leave the nest so suddenly, especially without licking the dishes clean, but the children put her back in a festive mood.

"Duke, you're such a mystery mouse," she chided. They were walking carefully down the icy foot bridge when she saw the large brick building before them.

"Oh, Duke!" she breathed.

It was not an easy trick to pass the five quints up to the hole in the brick, but everyone was in high spirits. The same glow lit the end of the mouseway. Melba was lightly trembling.

"You go first, Mother," Duke urged softly.

As Mother walked out on the molding, the lights played merrily on her shoulders and head. The children all gasped at her countenance as she turned to them in colored splendor.

"Oh, Duke," she whispered. "Oh, Duke." She marveled as she turned again to drink in the rich light.

"May-wy Cwis-mas!" chirped Quaid. The family rushed out to view the glory together. The mice danced with uninhibited joy in the rainbow of lights. They waltzed all along the molding, jumping, singing, and praising the light.

But all too soon the colors began to fade. Duke pulled Melba to sit beside him on the ledge of the molding. The rest of the family lined up on either side and watched quietly as the colors softened, faded, and then—were gone.

"Wow," whispered Elizabeth.

Duke started to round up the family for the trip home when the building filled with light. Not the mysteriously beautiful lights of color, but the bright lights of "There you are!" that men love to turn on mice. The mice froze in their tracks.

The building seemed to come alive instantly with dozens of humans and their children. No one was looking for the mice, but they were only three feet above the heads of the people, and in plain view.

"Don't move," Mother whispered without moving her mouth. Elizabeth became anxious and wanted to run, but Father held her paw firmly. She had half risen to go when the lights went on, and now, her knees were shaking in the half-crouched position. Father eased her to sit beside him.

Allister wasn't afraid. The rustle of the men and women excited his expectations. Somehow, he felt the humans who were here might know something about the sad man-child doll and the Light of which the Creator had spoken.

And regardless of how the mouse family felt, there was no escape now. The Spencers were captives for the Christmas Eve service.

The humans began singing. The sound

was wondrous. Rich melodious harmony swirled around the hall. The humans' voices nearly vibrated the Spencers off their perch.

"What are they singing?" Quade asked.

"I can't make it out," Mother said. "Something about a mother and child, I think."

Allister started. He strained so far forward to hear the words that Father pulled him back to safety. All Allister could understand was something about sleeping.

By this time, almost all of the people were sitting and looking away from the Spencers toward the front of the building, and the lights were turned low.

"I think we can leave now," whispered Mother.

"No!" Allister cried anxiously, causing a woman in the audience to turn and look behind her.

"Allister!" Mother scolded in a whisper, but Duke stopped her.

"Let him be, Melba. Something is happening here."

Allister's gaze riveted to a man stepping up to the front to face the crowd of people. He opened a big book and started to read, "In Luke it says, *And the angel said to her, 'Do not be afraid, Mary, for you have found favor with God. And behold, you will conceive in your womb and bear a Son, and you will call His name, Jesus.'*"

"'God' is what men call our Creator," Mother whispered to the quints.

The man stopped reading and looked up at the congregation of creatures. He readjusted his gaze through his trifocals several times as he spoke, "These words explain to us that Jesus was all man. Now listen to this passage in the book of Isaiah,

For to us a Child is born, to us a Son is given, and the government will be upon His shoulders, and His name will be called Wonderful Counselor, Mighty God, Everlasting Father, Prince of Peace."

Allister suddenly understood. The excitement inside his chest was bursting his lungs. "Do you see?" he coarsely whispered to his father. "Did you hear?"

Understanding was coming to Duke now, but was fuzzy. "Tell me," Duke encouraged.

"The man-child doll, the picture in lights...they are the...the Creator. He was here as a baby—a man's baby." The words brought a pure joy to Allister. The Creator's universe loomed far above him. This perfect plan, and Allister's place in it, brought him total contentment. He was the Creator's mousie and very grateful to be such.

Nothing could have broken into the space that Allister shared with his Creator except the reader's final offering. *"Arise, shine; for your Light has come!"*

Melba's head jerked up from her prayer. "Light?"

Joyous choruses filled the air around the Spencer family as they left, and the Light shown around them. No one spoke on the way home. The chill of the night and the crisp snow could not cool the hot joy of the evening in Allister's chest. He was glad to have the challenging run before him to employ the energy bursting inside.

The mouseways seemed hot and muggy when the Spencer family first came in. But as the family's walk slowed, the warmth became pleasant. The quints yawned and rubbed their beady eyes as they entered the cupboard. Quinn started to lift a sleepy leg into his manger bed when he stopped. He noticed the entire family was standing around the manger watching him.

"What?" he asked.

Allister and Elizabeth looked at their mother.

"Well, I didn't know He was a Creator-baby doll," she said in embarrassed protest.

Duke kissed Melba's cheek and went to the back corner of the box. He came back holding the doll as if it were a real mouse baby. He laid it carefully in the manger and then stepped back to join the admirers. The faces of the three wise men looked over Duke's shoulder, matching the awed expressions of the Spencers.

Allister suddenly wanted the picture complete. Using all his strength, he wrapped his front legs around the mother doll and heaved her next to the manger. Elizabeth got into the action and helped Allister wrangle the daddy doll to his post. They stepped back with the family to admire the scene.

Elizabeth began singing one of the Christmas songs learned from the third grade class that she had heard again tonight, "Silent Night! Holy Night!..."

The quints gathered in a circle and were whispering to each other, "Ooo! It's just like the light!"

Duke put his arm around Melba and pulled her to his side for a hug.

Allister moved quietly to the back of the cupboard and out to the mouseways. He had to talk to someone. Not another day could go by before he had an answer. But where would he find Julian?

Allister ran a switch, back and forth through the tunnels, as he thought. A feeling came over him to return to Cat's Crossing, the last place he had seen Julian. It was a long shot, but still, Allister went.

The crossing was empty when he arrived. This devastated Allister, and he wondered why. He crouched in the "head" formation of the intersection and felt miserable.

Then he heard something. Could it be?

"Allister," Julian said in greeting.

Allister jumped up and grabbed

Julian's arm to stop him. "Wait," Allister said. "I want to talk."

Julian nodded. He seemed to know that Allister was waiting for him. "What is it?"

"How did you know?" Allister asked.

Julian smiled. "Know what?"

Allister blinked and was afraid to ask, so he formed the words carefully. "About me. I didn't know. How did you?"

"Some mice are called to shine the Light. Some just aid the Light bearers. That's me. A helper."

Allister felt the warmth he knew from the roof-top experience seep through him again. He smiled. Then he said, "Now what?"

Julian laughed. "Now we shine, Buddy. We just shine." He gave Allister a light punch of friendship to his shoulder. "See you around," he said and loped off on his way. And Allister knew his adventure had just begun.

CPSIA information can be obtained
at www.ICGtesting.com
Printed in the USA
FSOW01n1410041114
3382FS